# STAR WARS™

## ADVENTURES IN
## WILD SPACE
### THE NEST

**Tom Huddleston**

A long time ago in a galaxy far, far away . . . .

## THE NEST

It is a time of darkness. With the
end of the Clone Wars and the
destruction of the Jedi Order, the
evil Emperor Palpatine rules the
galaxy unopposed.

After their parents are kidnapped by
the cruel Imperial Captain Korda,
Lina and Milo Graf flee into the
depths of Wild Space with only their
trusted droid CR-8R for company.

Just as all seems lost, the children
intercept a transmission calling for
a revolt against the Empire. Hoping
to find someone who can help them,
Milo and Lina set out to find the
source of the signal....

# CHAPTER 1

## THE DISTRESS CALL

'Come on, old girl,' Lina muttered as the *Whisper Bird* creaked and shuddered around them. 'You can do it.'

She couldn't help wondering what would happen if the ship came apart in hyperspace. Would they be trapped forever in this churning tunnel of light, or would they explode back into real space, a sudden flare in the blackness between the stars?

Lina sat bolt upright in the co-pilot's chair, alert to every rattle and groan. If anything went wrong it would be her own fault – disabling the hyperdrive safeties had been her idea. She could hear Morq chittering nervously in her brother's lap, and Milo whispering softly to keep the little Kowakian monkey-lizard calm.

Lina felt like she'd barely taken a breath since they blasted off from Thune. It had been a mistake to go there, she knew that now. The Empire had been waiting for them, ready to spring their trap.

But why? What were they carrying that was so valuable? CR-8R floated silently beside her, his lower limbs weaving in complex patterns as he scanned the navicomputer. Lina wished she knew what information their parents had uploaded into the old droid's circuits before the stormtroopers dragged them away.

She wished she knew why the Empire was so eager to get their hands on it. But most of all she wished she knew where her parents were, and what she could possibly do to get them back.

There was a sudden metallic snap from somewhere beneath them and Lina heard her brother gasp.

'It's nothing to worry about,' CR-8R said. 'A loose landing strut. The integrity of the hull has not been compromised.'

There was another pounding thud.

'Yet,' CR-8R added.

'How much longer?' Lina asked him.

'How much longer to the source of the transmission?' CR-8R replied. 'Or how much longer will the *Whisper Bird* hold together?'

'Both,' Lina and Milo said together.

'Not long,' CR-8R said. 'In either

case. But I don't believe there's any need to . . . wait.'

Lina craned to peer at the readout. Milo leaned in behind her, his hand squeezing her shoulder.

Without warning, the panel in front of CR-8R erupted in a spray of sparks. Lina covered her eyes as the smell of scorched metal filled the cabin. Morq let out a squeal.

The ship shook violently, then suddenly they were falling. Lina's stomach rolled over as the *Whisper Bird* tumbled, and she was thankful for the safety strap around her waist.

Through the viewscreen she could see stars, and the bright glow of a green world. They had dropped out of hyperspace.

'We have arrived,' CR-8R told them, his metal hands locked around

the steering controls. The panel still
sparked, the flashes reflected in his
black eyes. 'I apologise for the lack
of warning. Removing the safeties
somewhat confused the navicomputer.'

'Confused it?' Milo said. 'The
navicom blew up!'

CR-8R tapped the panel. 'It's only
an electrical short,' he said. 'Nothing I

can't fix. And it brought us here in one piece. Mostly.'

'What's the damage report?' Lina asked as the ship steadied.

'Minimal, surprisingly,' CR-8R told her. 'One shaky strut, and two of the power couplings on the hyperdrive have depolarised. They'll need to be replaced before we can make another jump.'

'You did it, sis,' Milo said, wrapping his arms around Lina's neck. 'You saved us.'

Lina flushed. 'I nearly killed us,' she said with a shudder. 'We took a risk and it paid off, but we can't keep relying on tricks and chance.'

'And I very much doubt this Captain Korda is going to stop looking for us any time soon,' CR-8R added. 'Whatever your parents transmitted into my memory banks, it appears to be highly valuable.'

'Well you still got us out of there,' Milo said appreciatively. 'And you managed to bring us here. Wherever here is.'

They peered through the viewscreen at the emerald orb below. The surface was wreathed in drifting cloud, but the sheer vibrant green shone through.

'Are you still picking up the transmission?' Lina asked. 'Can you lock on to the source?'

Milo tapped the screen set into the wall beside him, and a look of confusion crossed his face. 'That's odd,' he said. 'The signal's gone.'

Lina felt her heart plummet. 'But that's not possible,' she said. 'Crater, could the navicomputer have brought us to the wrong planet?'

The droid shook his gleaming head. 'The odds against a computer malfunction bringing us this close to a habitable world are approximately 3.76 million to one,' he said.

'Wait!' Milo said, pressing hard on his earpiece. 'I'm getting something. Let me try and boost the audio.'

He tapped the screen and a voice echoed through the cockpit, calm but insistent. '... reports continuing to come in of internment camps on multiple worlds,' the woman was saying, almost inaudible through waves of hissing feedback. 'On Kashyyyk, the Wookiees who fought so bravely against the Separatist army are now little more than slaves for the Empire.'

'And here's a transmission from Dinwa Prime,' the man cut in. 'Terrible atrocities have been committed in the name of the Emperor. We urge all people on these occupied worlds to . . . ' The signal faded back into static.

'So there is someone down there,' Lina said with relief. All their hopes were pinned on that mysterious signal. Someone out there was determined to resist the Empire. If anyone would be willing to help find their parents, surely it was them.

'I'm picking up massive life readings,' CR-8R said. 'But scans detect no evidence of major settlements and no other ships either on the ground or elsewhere in the system.'

'But a ship on the ground could be masked, couldn't it?' Lina asked. 'Whoever's sending the signal could be down there right now.'

'Or the Empire could already be here,' CR-8R pointed out. 'Trying to lure us into another trap.'

Lina glared at him. The droid was right, as usual. But sometimes she wished he would just keep his metal mouth shut.

'I don't think we have a choice,' Milo said. 'We won't get very far without a functioning hyperdrive.'

Lina's own words echoed in her head – could they really keep trusting luck? But Milo was right, they were out of options.

She tightened her seat strap. 'Take us down slowly, Crater. And be prepared to run at the first sign of trouble.'

The droid hesitated, then he gripped the steering control. 'I have a bad feeling about this.'

It was Milo who spotted the settlement. It stood perched on the crest of a high, rocky ridge overlooking

a thickly forested valley – a broad,
low-roofed building with sheer metal
sides and floor-to-ceiling windows
reflecting the pale light of the rising
sun. It was wreathed in shifting mist
and surrounded by a defensive wall
that towered over the structure itself.

'It looks new,' Lina observed. 'And
sort of expensive.'

She was right. The main settlement was built of black durasteel, the flat roof painted with the golden symbol of a hunting bird, its wings spread wide. A glass platform jutted over the ridge, offering spectacular views of the valley below. A fast-flowing stream had been diverted into channels around the central building, creating a pair of magnificent waterfalls that gushed over the cliff and sparkled into the jungle below.

'The signal's getting stronger,' Milo reported. 'That has to be the source.'

'But I don't understand,' Lina said. 'Why would the person who sent those transmissions live in a place like this? Whoever built it isn't trying to hide from anyone.'

'It's hideous,' Crater agreed. 'Precisely the kind of garish, tasteless display one would expect from an Outer Rim trader or a successful spice mine owner, not a revolutionary.'

'We're so far out in Wild Space,' Milo offered. 'Maybe they think no one will come looking for them. Let's fly lower, maybe we'll get some answers.'

They descended slowly, CR-8R angling the thrusters to get a better look. A broad track led from a gate in the perimeter wall, weaving down through the jungle to a large rectangular clearing on the hillside below. A landing strip.

'Is that a ship?' Milo asked, pointing.

CR-8R focused the scanner. 'It was,' he said. 'What a mess.'

Lina peered through the viewscreen. At the base of a narrow ravine between the landing field and the main structure she could make out a black shape, the square metal frame of a transport. One wing hung limp at the side, the other was nowhere to be seen.

The surrounding trees had been shattered and uprooted, but there were no scorch marks. It was as if the ship had been ripped to pieces and tossed aside.

'Could that wreck have the parts we need?' Milo asked.

'It's possible,' Lina admitted. 'But we'd have to set down on the landing strip and make our way to the crash site on foot.'

'We still have no idea what happened here,' CR-8R pointed out. 'What if someone blasted that ship out of the sky?'

'The scans found no nearby ships,' Lina objected. 'And we can set the *Whisper Bird* to alert us if it picks up so much as a stray asteroid in the area.'

'And remember the signal,' Milo pointed out. 'That's why we're out here, we should at least try to find the source.'

Lina nodded. 'Agreed. Once we're on the ground I can rig up my comlink to track it.'

CR-8R angled the stick reluctantly. 'As you wish,' he said. 'But if we all end up dead, don't say I didn't warn you.'

# CHAPTER 2

## THE WRECKED SHIP

An eerie silence hung over the landing field as they hurried down the *Whisper Bird*'s ramp. The air was hot and hazy, a thin mist hugging the muddy ground.

The landing strip had been hacked from the jungle, a short expanse of close-cropped grass with a low wooden shack at the far end. Beside it Milo could see the track that led up to the settlement, winding into the trees. He hoped they'd get the chance to explore properly once they'd checked the wreck for parts.

CR-8R drifted ahead of them, a murky shape in the gloom. Lina and Milo followed, their boots squelching. Morq clung to Milo's shoulder, chirruping nervously, his tail twitching and slapping on the boy's back.

'Look,' Milo said, spotting a patch of scorched yellow grass flattened by four large, flat circles. 'The ship must have taken off from here, then for some reason it crashed.'

'Engine failure?' Lina asked.

'It is possible,' CR-8R agreed. He paused for a moment. 'I'm not sure it's wise for us all to go wandering off into the jungle. Perhaps someone should stay with the ship.'

'That might not be a bad idea,' Lina said, and Milo saw the flicker of a smile cross her face. 'Crater, you press on ahead and check out that crash, you can radio back to us here.'

'Great plan, Sis,' Milo agreed. 'After all, one of us could get hurt. A droid is much more durable.'

CR-8R spun around to face them. 'I know you think you're being funny,' he said. 'But I don't appreciate it. Not one bit.'

'Don't worry, Crater,' Lina grinned. 'We wouldn't let you go off alone. Anyway, I don't like the thought of splitting up. This planet's creepy enough as it is.'

CR-8R nodded. 'If you insist.'

The shadows deepened as they pushed into the trees. Leafy limbs arced overhead, blocking out the watery sun.

A swarm of tiny blue insects spiralled into the light, their nest disturbed by Lina's blundering feet. The air was

damp and filled with the musty smell
of rotting wood.

Morq hunkered on Milo's shoulder,
peering around nervously. The boy
was surprised. The little monkey-
lizard should have been off exploring,
scampering up the trees after ripe fruit

and unguarded eggs. Something must have spooked him, but Milo had no idea what it could be.

They paused on the bank of a rocky stream and Lina crouched, splashing her face. Dead leaves spiralled in the clear water and giant webs shimmered in the half-light, jewelled with moisture.

Somewhere high above they heard the cry of a hunting bird, piercing the still air. Milo realised that aside from the chirp and hum of insects, this was the first animal call he'd heard since they touched down. This forest was so quiet, it was starting to become unsettling.

'Something has been this way ahead of us,' CR-8R said, floating onto the far bank. 'This tree trunk did not snap in two by itself.'

'You sure it wasn't the wind or something?' Milo asked, hopping from rock to rock across the shallow brook. 'If some creature did it, it's keeping awfully qui–'

'AHOOOOOOOOOOOOOOOOO . . .'

An unearthly howl rose all around them, its source impossible to pinpoint in the thick jungle. The sound grew louder, and louder still – then suddenly it stopped, and the silence fell once more.

'My bad feeling just got a lot worse,' CR-8R said, cranking his vocabulator down a few notches.

Lina dried her face on her sleeve. 'Milo, do you have any idea what that was?'

He shook his head. 'It sounded big.'

'And angry,' CR-8R agreed. 'Might I suggest we get what we came for, then essay a precipitous departure?'

'If you mean we should grab what we need and run,' Lina nodded, 'that sounds like a great plan.'

They left the stream, scrambling down a last rocky incline to the base of the ravine. The wrecked ship loomed over them.

Milo peered up, making out the word

*Venture* branded on the ship's side. It was the kind of craft that was common in the Outer Rim – a bulky freighter built for transporting heavy loads.

But he doubted it would ever fly again. The nearside wing was almost completely severed, black cables exposed. The landing gear had crumpled, causing the body of the ship to list towards them at a steep angle. And three twisted gashes ran the length of the hull, from the cockpit to the rear-loading hatch. They almost look like claw marks, Milo thought. But that was impossible.

CR-8R rose on his repulsors, peering through the mud-streaked windows. 'It seems deserted,' he reported. 'The pilot must have abandoned ship.'

The droid glided down, landing gently on the roof. The metal groaned and shifted, but only a little. 'It's stable,' he told them. 'You can climb on up, both of you.'

Milo took hold of a dangling cable, hauling himself into the rear hangar before turning to help Lina up. CR-8R drifted through the jagged hole in the roof, activating his glowlamps. Morq scampered down from Milo's shoulder, squirrelling his way into a pile of scrap and hiding there, peering out.

'Are these cages?' Lina asked, gesturing to a twisted steel frame hanging against the far wall. She peered closer, then drew back. 'Milo, check it out.'

Slumped in the bottom of the cage was a large figure, a creature perhaps twice the size of a man. Its thick brown fur was almost black in the light of CR-8R's beams. Milo couldn't help noticing the blood on its jagged white claws.

Lina reached out with one cautious foot, nudging the cage. The creature did not stir.

'I think it's dead,' Milo whispered.

CR-8R swept one of his lower limbs past the cage, a faint blue light flickering over the still form. 'My bio-scanners confirm it,' he said.

'It looks like some kind of primate,' Milo said, crouching beside the cage. The creature lay sprawled on its side with its mouth open, revealing rows of yellow teeth. 'A veermok, or close to it. But they're native to Naboo, what's it doing here?'

'And more importantly, what could have done that to it?' Lina asked.

'I don't mean to alarm you,' CR-8R said, gesturing. 'But look here.'

A second cage lay twisted in the shadows, its bars bent wide. Around it, the floor of the hangar was torn and clawed, spattered with black droplets.

Milo touched one of the drops, his fingers coming away red. 'There must have been two creatures,' he said. 'Maybe one got loose and attacked the other.'

'It could still be around,' CR-8R said, spinning round. 'Perhaps it was responsible for that awful howl.'

'Veermoks may be strong,' Milo observed. 'But those are durasteel bars. I don't see how they could do this kind of damage.'

'Look, I don't know what's going on,' Lina said firmly. 'This place just keeps getting weirder. But we came here for a reason. Crater, can you get up front and see if there's anything we can use?'

'Of course, Mistress Lina,' CR-8R said, using his powerful load-lifting arm to clear a path towards the cockpit.

Milo followed, ducking under a leaning hull plate. He could hear Morq scrabbling around nearby, squawking to himself. Then the monkey-lizard scuttled towards him, clutching something in his talons.

'What have you got there?' Milo asked, crouching. 'Come on, drop it.'

Morq did as he was told, peering eagerly up at the boy. It was a boot. Milo turned it over in his hands thoughtfully. Could it have belonged to the pilot? And if so, where was he?

Milo tossed the shoe aside and Morq darted after it, ripping the leather to pieces with his beak and swallowing it. 'Oh, come on,' Milo said. 'You don't know where that's been. Put it down.'

Morq looked up at him and squeaked defensively. He backed away, scuttling up the side of the loose hull-plate, which shuddered beneath his weight.

'Morq, careful,' Milo said. 'You don't want to–'

With a crash the plate toppled, missing Milo by centimetres as the sharp edge sliced into the floor. The boy sprang back, his heart pounding. Morq let out a screech and jumped clear, the boot forgotten.

'What did I just say?' Milo spat. 'I could've been squashed.'

Morq flattened his ears, letting out an apologetic squeak.

'If your little friend has finished wreaking maximum havoc,' CR-8R's voice came from the other side of the barrier. 'I have good news and bad news. Which would you like first?'

'Good, I guess,' Lina shrugged.

'The good news is that the cockpit is largely undamaged,' the droid said. 'The hyperdrive appears to be in one piece, and the couplings should be compatible.'

'That's great,' Lina called out. 'What's the bad news?'

'I've been able to communicate with the ship's computer,' CR-8R reported.
'It didn't like me prying around. These old freighters can be so rude. If you could have heard some of the language it was . . . '

'What did it tell you, Crater?' Lina cut in impatiently.

'It told me, in no uncertain terms, that the crash was not a result of engine failure, or of anything inside the ship. Not it's fault, in other words.'

'Why is that bad news?' Milo asked.

'Because of the final report from the external sensors,' CR-8R told him. 'The *Venture* was struck in the side, a physical blow that knocked the craft out of the sky.'

'A laser blast?' Milo asked.

'I didn't see any scorch marks,' Lina said. 'Just those weird scars on the outside of the ship.'

'It is my belief that– wait,' CR-8R said sharply. 'I'm receiving a signal from the *Whisper Bird*. Another ship just came out of hyperspace above the planet.'

Milo tried to reach the cockpit but the fallen hull plate blocked his path. 'Imperial?' he asked.

'Uncertain,' CR-8R replied from within. 'The model does not appear to be in my records. But a shuttle has just detached from the main ship, and is descending fast.'

'The Empire,' Lina said decisively. 'They've found us. Crater, move your circuits.'

There was a grind of metal, CR-8R's servers straining as he tried to shift the plate that Morq had brought down. But it was wedged fast.

'It's too heavy,' CR-8R's voice sounded. 'I shall have to cut through. Both of you, go.'

'I won't leave you,' Lina insisted. 'What if the stormtroopers find you?'

'I will disguise myself as part of the wreckage,' CR-8R said. 'It shouldn't be too hard.'

Milo peered into the murky sky. He could see a black speck high above them, getting bigger. His heart pounded.

Morq squealed, running towards him. Milo shooed him away. He'd be safer here than out in the jungle. 'Stay, boy,' he said. 'Look after Crater.'

'I'll keep him safe,' the droid called out. 'Now Master Milo please, run. Before it's too late.'

Milo dropped into the dirt, dashing after Lina into the trees.

# CHAPTER 3

## THE LODGE

Lina and Milo clambered up the rocky slope, back into the jungle. The rumble of engines sounded out behind them. Lina glanced back, peering through a gap in the branches as a shadow fell over the wrecked ship. The trees shook and they shielded their eyes as a wave of heat rolled over them.

A sleek, blunt-nosed shuttle descended towards the crash site, black and gold with platinum bearings and eight ion engines. It looked top of the line, every bit as expensive as the settlement they'd seen from the air.

Lina felt a wave of relief crash
over her. This was no Imperial vessel.
Through the glass of the cockpit she
could make out a tall figure bent over
the controls.

The thrusters fired and the ship
hovered above the wreck. The rear

hatch slid back and two figures emerged, crouching on the edge. One was slender and clad in black, face covered by a close-fitting mask that looked strangely familiar. The other was shorter and heavier, gripping the side of the shuttle as they descended.

The tall one jumped first, landing upright on the roof of the wrecked ship with practised ease. The second was more ungainly, dropping awkwardly and rolling on his back. The first figure looked around, scanning the treeline.

Lina jerked back into the shadows, cursing her own foolishness. She could easily have been spotted. Just because they weren't stormtroopers didn't mean these newcomers weren't dangerous.

They scrabbled up the slope,

leaves stinging their faces as they ran. Lina heard the ship rising again, and glancing up she saw it streak overhead, back towards the landing strip. So much for getting back to the *Bird* unseen.

There was a muffled crackling sound. 'Mistress Lina,' a voice said, startling her. 'Mistress Lina, can you hear me?'

Lina reached into her pocket, pulling out her little comlink. 'Crater, what's happening?'

'I am still inside the *Venture*'s cockpit,' the droid's voice came back. 'Two people have entered and are inspecting the wreck.'

'Don't let them hear you,' Milo warned.

'Don't worry, Master Milo,' CR-8R told him. 'I have disconnected my exterior vocabulator and linked directly with the comlink.'

'Smart,' Milo grinned.

'Could you also reroute your aural sensors?' Lina asked. That way we can hear their conversation.'

'Good idea, Mistress Lina,' CR-8R agreed. 'I'll do so now.'

There was a click and a long silence. Then they heard the distinct sound of footsteps.

'Someone's definitely been here,' a man's voice came through, dull and echoing. 'Look, boss. A shoe.'

'That's Meggin's boot, laser-brain,' a woman snapped, her voice muffled. 'I'd recognise those clodhoppers anywhere. But you're right, whoever landed in that craft has been poking around in here. I can smell them.'

Lina felt an involuntary shudder.

She knew they probably stank of Thunian bugspray, but still, that was unnatural.

Then she remembered the mask the woman had been wearing. She knew she'd seen one like it before, and now she recalled where. On that trip to Ikari about a year ago, the village elder had owned a mask that allowed him to see, hear and smell more acutely than any of the other tribesmen. It had made him a fearsome hunter.

'Corin,' the woman was saying. 'What news on the other craft?'

'No sign of life,' a crackling voice came back. 'It is half a wreck also. The hyperdrive is badly damaged.'

'Scavengers,' the woman said. 'Looking for spare parts on my ship. But who would be scavenging all the way out here?'

'And why would they do this to the *Venture*?' the first man asked.

'Don't be a fool, Bort,' the woman said. 'This damage was not their doing. Look, these are clearly claw marks. This was the work of one of Meggin's monsters.'

'Do you think it's still out here?' her companion asked, and Lina could hear just a hint of worry in his voice.

The woman snorted. 'Don't be so pathetic,' she growled. 'I thought you were supposed to be mercenaries, the worst scum in the galaxy. You told me you were wanted on seven systems, you're surely not afraid of some lumbering beast with more teeth than brain cells.'

'Yes, boss,' the man said uncertainly.

'Now let's head down to the landing field and take a look at that ship,' the

woman went on. 'These scavengers
won't get away with it.'

'What are you going to do?' the man
asked.

'Do I have to spell everything out for
you?' the woman sighed. 'Blast them,
of course.'

They heard footsteps retreating,
then CR-8R's voice cut back in.

'Well, she seemed most unfriendly,'
he said. 'And I'm afraid her companion
didn't look much better. He wasn't
a large man, but he appeared to be
carrying a blaster approximately the
size of Master Milo.'

'So what do we do now?' Milo asked.
'We can't get back to the *Bird*, they'll be
waiting for us.'

'Then there's only one place
to go,' Lina said. 'We follow that
transmission. It's our only hope.'

Lina and Milo pushed through a last wall of trees and found themselves on the edge of a broad, grassy track. The same one they'd seen as they circled in, Lina knew – if they followed it uphill, they'd soon reach the settlement.

They trudged up the slope, shielding their eyes from the sun. The building stood hunched on the horizon, the black roof curving away from them, shrouded in vapour from the waterfalls on either side. Below it stood the perimeter fence, higher than all but the tallest trees and made from sheer durasteel, an impenetrable protective wall.

Except that something had managed to penetrate it. On the side furthest from the track a great hole had been torn, a jagged tear stretching from the top of the fence almost to the ground. The steel had been pulled back, like a sheet of paper folded over by a giant hand. Lina saw three huge scratches in the steel and remembered the marks on the *Venture*'s hull.

'What could have done this?' she asked Milo as they approached.

He shook his head in wonder. 'I have no idea,' he admitted. 'But whatever it is, it must be big.'

They climbed cautiously through the gap in the fence, alert to any movement. Lina drew out her comlink, scanning the radio band. The transmission faded in and out, but it was strongest when she pointed it directly at the structure up ahead.

'... Empire will do everything they can to hunt us down,' the woman was saying, her voice loud in the jungle stillness. 'But we will stand firm, resisting all efforts to . . . '

Lina clicked off the comlink. 'This has to be the place.'

As they crept forward she became aware of a rotten smell on the air, like a blend of marsh gas and rotting meat. She saw Milo covering his nose and grimacing.

'What is that?' Lina asked. 'It's revolting.'

'It's this goop everywhere,' Milo observed. 'I wonder what could've made it?'

Lina had noticed the pale, glutinous liquid spattered on the grass, but she hadn't thought to connect it with the foul smell.

'Just when you think this planet can't get any stranger,' she said, skirting a large puddle of the stuff.

'You haven't seen anything yet,' Milo

whispered. 'Look.'

Lina raised her head and had to stifle a gasp. From the air, they'd only been able to make out the front of the black structure – the plate glass windows, the durasteel roof. The rest had been shrouded in mist. If they had seen it, she thought, they might have thought twice about landing.

It looked like something had taken a bite out of the place – the rear side was little more than rubble, a twisted mess of shattered wood and tortured steel. The roof had been peeled back just like the perimeter fence, and the windows were shattered from floor to ceiling.

'I'm starting to think this was a bad idea,' Milo whispered.

'Me too,' Lina said. 'Are you saying you want to go back?'

Milo shook his head. 'I don't hear anything moving about,' he said. 'I think whatever did this is gone. And we have to find the source of that signal.'

'But how are we supposed to get inside?' Lina asked, peering up at the tangled ruin.

'Down there,' Milo suggested indicating a narrow shaft in the ground, set apart from the worst of the destruction. 'It must lead down to a cellar of some kind. Maybe we can go under, and back up.'

Lina saw metal steps leading down into the earth. She scanned with her comlink. The signal was still coming through loud and clear.

They were almost to the steps when a sudden movement made them look up. A heap of bricks toppled to the ground, followed by the faintest chittering noise and a blast of that ripe, foul smell.

'There's something here,' Lina said, and Milo nodded.

'I thought I saw it before,' he agreed. 'Some kind of rodent, I think. No bigger than hand-sized. It didn't look dangerous.'

Lina frowned. 'Well if something tries to bite me, I'm blaming you.'

A door at the base of the steps stood open and Milo pushed through. On the other side was a large six-sided room, its low steel walls lined with banks of computer terminals and flickering monitor screens.

White lights flickered on automatically as they entered, but the room was deserted. Like everywhere else on this planet, Lina thought. In the centre was a deep pit and they peered

over the edge, gripping the handrail.
Pale blue light emanated from below,
and she heard a deep, juddering thrum.
A power source.

'This must be the control centre,'
Lina said. 'Look, here are the lights,
heating, security systems. But I don't
see the communications linkup. There
must be a second hub, somewhere else
in the building.'

They left the room through a
narrow entranceway on the far side,
finding themselves in a long concrete
corridor with buzzing lights set into
the ceiling. Through a hatch in the
wall they could see an enormous
kitchen, a maze of gleaming metal
surfaces. Everything looked spotless
and unused.

An imposing pair of wooden
doors stood facing them, the left one

standing open. Milo stepped through, and his mouth dropped open. 'Woah, look at this,' he said.

They were standing on the edge of a huge, high-ceilinged room floored with dark, varnished wood. A massive chandelier hung overhead, sparkling with gold and glass. But that wasn't what had drawn Milo's attention.

From floor to roof and from end to end, the walls were lined with animal heads of every size and species imaginable. From furry nexu to scaly dewbacks, from the magnificent plumage of a varactyl to the savage grimace of a rancor, creatures from every sector of the galaxy had been stuffed, mounted and put on display.

Some of the smaller specimens had been kept intact – Lina saw a mynock suspended from the ceiling, its wings spread in flight. And there was a rearing narglatch, claws bared as though ready to attack. Their glassy eyes seemed to stare at Lina, and all she could do was stare back.

She pulled the comlink from her pocket, but Milo grabbed her arm. 'Don't switch it on,' he hissed urgently.

'Why not?' Lina asked.

'Because of that,' Milo said, and pointed a trembling finger.

Lina looked, but all she could see was another one of those stuffed creatures, huge and hairy with sharp teeth and hazy, bloodshot eyes.

'What?' she said. 'I don't see any–'

The creature blinked.

Lina jumped backwards, hitting the wall and biting back a cry of surprise.

'Stay still,' Milo hissed. 'Maybe it won't see us.'

Lina froze, clutching his hand. The words of the masked woman echoed in her head. What had she said? 'Meggin's monsters'?

'It's a veermok,' Milo whispered. 'This must be the one that escaped, back at the *Venture*.'

'Are they aggressive?' Lina asked.

Milo nodded. 'Very.'

The creature on the ship had looked almost pitiable, sprawled like rags on the floor of the cage. But this veermok was very much alive, huge teeth snapping as it eyed them keenly.

It took a step forward, sniffing the air. It had powerful black forearms, thumping on the boards as it took another step towards them. Then the veermok lowered its head.

'Go!' Milo cried, grabbing Lina and shoving her back into the corridor.

They heard the bellow and stamp as
the creature thundered after them, its
huge fists splintering the floorboards.

They hurtled back along the hall
and into the control room, sprinting
around the central pit towards the

steps on the far side. The veermok shoved through the narrow doorway, roaring as its broad shoulders were momentarily wedged. Then it shook its massive body and the door frame shattered, raining masonry and splinters down on the beast as it fought free.

Lina followed Milo up into the light, glancing back to see the veermok springing over the central pit in a single bound. But as she reached the top of the steps her foot slipped in a puddle of that foul goo and she fell.

Lina cried out as she hit the floor, expecting at any moment to feel the creature's paw tightening around her ankle.

But it never came. She rolled onto her back, lifting her head. The veermok had paused at the base of the steps, peering out into the light.

For the first time, Lina saw that its fur was matted with blood. A ragged wound ran from its neck right along its arm, as though something had lashed at it with sharp claws. There were more marks on its chest and legs.

The veermok eyes were red and damp. There was something in them, Lina thought. Something more than just hunger and fury. Could it be fear? But what could possibly scare a beast this size?

The veermok lowered its head, taking a tentative step out into the light. Lina knew she should clamber up, should try to run. But she also knew it was no use. They were out in the open now, there was nowhere left to hide.

The veermok lumbered to the top of

the steps, looming over her. Lina drew back, holding her breath. Milo let out a gasp.

A blaster shot rang out. The veermok jerked back, a look of befuddlement crossing its features.

Then it fell, toppling forward like a falling tree. Lina rolled clear just in time as the beast crashed face-first into the rubble.

She heard footsteps, turning to see a figure in black striding towards them, a rifle raised to her eye. A golden bird was emblazoned across her chest, wings spread.

The woman lowered the rifle and unclipped the sensor mask, red hair tumbling around her pale, pitiless face. She looked down at the veermok, a smile of satisfaction playing across her lips.

Then she turned to Lina and Milo, her eyes an ice-cold blue.

'Who are you,' she demanded. 'And what are you doing on *my* planet?'

# CHAPTER 4

## STINKERS

'Move,' the red-haired woman growled, gesturing with her rifle. She marched Milo and Lina through the rubble to where a pale figure stood waiting.

'They are merely children,' he wheezed as they approached. He was tall and gaunt, with greyish skin and red-rimmed eyes. A Pau'an mercenary, Milo realised with a shudder. What had the woman called him? Corin?

'But what are they doing out here?' The third man came striding towards them, his face gleaming with sweat.

'Did you ask them that?' Slung over
his shoulder was the biggest blaster
Milo had ever seen. This must be
Bort.

The woman looked expectantly at

the children. 'Answer him,' she said. 'What gives you the right to land on my planet?'

Lina snorted defiantly. 'No one owns a whole planet.'

The woman bristled. 'This is Wild Space. Out here, whatever you find, you keep. I found Xirl, and I intend to keep it. My name is Gozetta, and out here, I'm the boss. So I ask again, what are your names, and what are you doing here?'

'Don't tell her anything, Lina,' Milo hissed. Then he gulped, realising what he'd said.

Gozetta smiled thinly. 'Lina, is it?' she asked. 'And what's your name, little one?'

Milo considered inventing something, then realised it probably wouldn't make a lot of difference.

'Milo,' he told her. 'And I'm not that little.'

The woman laughed. 'A brave boy,' she said. 'Your parents must be proud. Where are they?' She scanned the treeline.

'They're out hunting,' Milo said. 'They'll be here any minute. And the rest of our party. They took all the weapons and went to catch supper.'

'Sorry, kid, I don't think so,' Gozetta said. 'I saw your ship. A four-person craft. And you both look . . . lost. What parent would allow you to dress in such filthy rags? I could've picked up your scent a kilometre away, even without this.' She gestured to the mask clipped to her collar.

'Just let us go,' Lina said. 'We'll leave this place and never come back, I promise.'

Gozetta's eyes narrowed. 'With no hyperdrive? No, you're up to something and I intend to find out what. It's no coincidence that you show up just as my people go mysteriously missing, and all this happens.' She gestured at the devastation surrounding them.

'What could have done it?' Milo asked, unable to stop himself.

Gozetta shook her head. 'It's a long list,' she said. 'You see, this planet isn't quite like any other.'

'You mean the creatures?' Milo asked. 'That was a veermok back there, wasn't it?'

Gozetta inspected him keenly. 'Sharp little thing, aren't you?' she said. 'Yes, you're right. At last count I have two of them, plus two rancors, a krayt dragon and four gundarks. They must be the ones responsible for the damage to the Venture, those things have quite a leap.'

'I never heard of gundarks attacking a ship in flight before,' Milo said. 'On the ground, maybe, but the *Venture* had already blasted off. And besides, it'd take thirty gundarks to make that hole in your fence.'

The woman shrugged. 'Biology's not my specialty,' she said. 'Meggin's the man for that. It's his job to keep them alive, I . . . do the opposite.'

'You hunt them,' Lina said, realisation flooding over her. The mask, the cages, it all made sense. 'We saw all those heads in there. This is your hunting lodge, isn't it? You're bringing these animals here, then you're going to go out and kill them.'

Gozetta put up her hands. 'You got

me,' she said. 'I am a hunter, just like my father and his father. Those heads are the result of a lifetime's work, on a hundred worlds.'

'My dad told me game hunting was big business,' Milo said. 'For anyone mean and cowardly enough to want to do it.'

'Smart man,' Gozetta agreed. 'I have come to despise those tourist reserves. Under constant guard, only shooting what they allow you to shoot. That's not hunting, it's child's play.'

She gazed out across the tree-covered hills. 'Here it's just me and them. No one tells me what or when or how to kill. When I'm done, this planet will be crawling with critters, breeding and thriving and ready for the hunt. Xirl is the perfect world for it, too. There's no indigenous life bigger than a tree snake.'

'And you're sure about that?' Milo asked, looking again at the hole in the fence.

Gozetta's face darkened. 'Like I said,' she snarled. 'Gundarks.' But he could tell she wasn't convinced.

There was a sudden scrabbling noise from behind them and Gozetta whipped round, drawing her rifle. A shot rang out and she smiled coldly. 'Got you.'

She strode to the top of a pile of rubble, Milo close on her heels. A small creature lay on its back, feet in the air. It was about as long as Milo's forearm, with scaly skin and a long, segmented neck topped by a triangular head.

'Did you have to kill it?' Milo asked

the woman accusingly.

She shrugged. 'I told you, kid. That's what I do.' She nudged the creature with her toe, wrinkling her nose. 'I guess we know where that disgusting smell's been coming from.'

Milo crouched. 'It must secrete that sticky stuff to mark its territory,' he said. 'I wonder where you came from, little friend. And if there are any more of you around.'

'Um, look up,' Lina said, and Milo lifted his head.

On the far side of the lodge stood a tall structure, wide at the base and narrow at the top, tipped with a long silver spire. For a moment Milo thought it was alive, the whole surface seemed to be writhing. Then he realised that every centimetre was covered in the little creatures, swarming over each other like insects in a hive.

'I think I'm going to be sick,' Bort said, staring in horrified fascination.

The structure had begun to lean beneath the creatures' combined weight, the metal struts groaning.

'Is that what I think it is?' Milo whispered, leaning close to his sister.

'A transmission beacon,' Lina nodded. 'Did you hear Gozetta before? She said my people. There must have been others working at the lodge.'

'Get out of here!' The huntress strode towards the tower with her rifle raised, squeezing off three shots in rapid succession. Several creatures dropped dead in the dirt but the rest ignored her, scurrying up and down the creaking structure. 'Horrid little stinkers!' Gozetta shouted, and fired again.

'Boss, are you sure that's wise?'
Bort asked. 'That thing doesn't look
too stable.'

Gozetta ignored him, blasting
furiously. They heard a shot strike
the metal of the tower and it let out a

long, grinding groan.

Gozetta sprang clear as the beacon toppled, flattening more of the creatures beneath it and sending up a cloud of dust.

For a moment there was silence. Then Gozetta let out a scream of fury and frustration.

'I have had enough of this!' she cried, stamping her feet in the dirt. 'I've spent months building this place, I spent all of my credits . . .' She raised her rifle, firing blindly into the air. 'This is my planet,' she cried at the top of her voice.

Lina pulled the comlink from her pocket, but it emitted nothing but static. 'So we know the signal came from that tower,' she said in a low voice.

'Now we just have to figure out who

sent it,' Milo agreed.

'All of you, look,' Corin's voice rang out. The dust was beginning to clear, and through it they could see past the wreck of the transmission tower to where a second, even larger hole had been torn in the perimeter fence. Beyond it, a trail of devastation and shattered trees led along the ridge and into the jungle.

As they watched, the creatures swarming over the tower began to spring free, heading towards the gap in the fence.

'Where are they all going?' Bort asked, scratching his head.

'I don't know,' Gozetta said, her eyes narrow. 'But something tells me that trail is going to lead directly to whatever trashed my lodge.'

'You no longer suspect the

gundarks?' Corin asked.

Gozetta shook her head. 'The boy's right,' she said. 'Nothing I shipped in could do this kind of damage. It must have been here all along, we just didn't see it.'

'This thing brought down a whole ship and ripped a hole in a durasteel fence,' Bort objected. 'Two holes, in fact. It must be big.'

'Undoubtedly,' Gozetta said, shouldering her rifle. 'But it's like I said before, I found this place and I intend to keep it. I won't let some dumb animal come in here and take it from me.'

'So what are you going to do?' Milo asked.

'What my father taught me,' Gozetta said proudly. 'I'm going to hunt, I'm going to trap, and I'm going to kill. So saddle up, because you're all coming with me.'

# CHAPTER 5

## THE CAVE

'I don't like this, Mistress Lina,' CR-8R's voice came rattling through the comlink. 'I don't like it one bit.'

'Neither do I, Crater,' Lina whispered. 'But what are we supposed to do? They may not be the Empire, but they still have blasters.'

'As long as you and Master Milo are safe,' the droid said.

'He's fine,' Lina said. 'I think he's actually starting to enjoy himself. All these new life forms to discover. I told him to keep that woman distracted so I could talk to you.'

She glanced up the slope to where

Milo and Gozetta were picking through the jungle, or what was left of it. The creature had left a swathe of destruction, uprooting trees and digging great furrows in the earth. And the little stinkers had followed, their foul stench hanging in the hot, dry air.

Lina could see a group of them now, chattering to one another as they dragged what appeared to be an entire leg of cured bantha meat along the shattered trail. They had raided Gozetta's larder, and the forest was littered with half-chewed fruit and empty plastic packets. She couldn't help thinking of that old story her mother used to tell, about the children who followed a trail of candy into the woods and got themselves in bad trouble.

'Well I do have some news,' the droid

told her. 'I have managed to cut myself free, and am about to begin ferrying the hyperdrive parts back to the *Whisper Bird.*'

'That's great,' Lina grinned. 'How long will the repairs take?'

'Several hours,' CR-8R told her. 'Longer if Master Milo's furry companion doesn't stop getting in my way.'

'Morq's okay, then?' Lina asked.

'Unfortunately, yes,' CR-8R said ruefully. 'My fervent wish that he might encounter another loose hull plate remains unanswered.'

'Crater,' Lina laughed, 'don't be awful.'

'Hey,' a voice sounded from up the track, and Lina's head shot up. Bort gestured with his gigantic blaster. 'Pick up the pace.'

Lina shot him her most innocent smile. 'Right behind you,' she called out. 'I'm just a kid, remember?'

The short man frowned, but he turned his back and trudged after the others.

'I'll be in touch,' Lina whispered. 'Make what repairs you can. We'll be back soon, I promise.' Then she clicked off the comlink and hurried after the others.

'Just a kid,' Bort said as she drew alongside. 'I've heard that before. My little girl used to say it, right before she dropped me in the biggest heap of trouble . . .' He broke off, smiling to himself.

'You have a daughter?' Lina asked, surprised.

'What, you don't think mercenaries have families?' Bort asked. 'She's going to the Academy this year. Officer training.' There was pride in his voice, and just a hint of doubt.

'I bet she'll do great,' Lina assured him.

'Sure she will,' Bort grunted. 'The Empire knows what's best for all of us.' He fell silent for a moment, gazing off into the trees. 'Come on, let's catch up to the boss.'

'. . . and I thought it seemed strange that this planet had no top predator,' Milo was telling Gozetta as Lina jogged up behind them. 'Every ecosystem ought to have one, right?'

'I suppose so,' Gozetta said thoughtfully. 'But why didn't it show up on my bio-scans? And why haven't we seen it before now? It took weeks to build the lodge, and we didn't see a thing.'

'I've got a theory about that,' Milo said brightly.

'Of course you have,' Gozetta muttered.

'Back at the lodge,' Milo explained, 'those . . . whatever they are, those stinkers, they were all over your transmission tower. If the little ones and the big one are related somehow, maybe it was drawn to the tower too, like they were. Maybe there's something in the signal that draws them, like sonar.'

Gozetta nodded. 'Communications only went online last week,' she said. 'Sata, my tech expert, was running some tests.'

'That would explain it,' Milo said, and he shot Lina a pointed look. They needed to find this Sata. If she was still alive.

The air grew thinner as they climbed, leaving the clouds behind and ascending towards a high plateau of black volcanic rock that thrust its head from the surrounding jungle. The sun beat down, and Lina could feel the sweat coursing down her back.

All around them she could hear the chatter of stinkers and smell their rank odour. She saw now that it wasn't just Gozetta's larder they'd helped themselves to – the creatures were hauling everything from medkits to hydrospanners, the shinier the better. One particularly well organised group were carrying an entire dinner service, a line of golden plates and goblets bobbing their way up the trail.

Two stinkers were fighting over a filthy, ripped-up shoe, hissing and growling at one another. One lashed out at the other, snatching its prize and guarding it ferociously.

'Have you noticed there are two different kinds?' Milo asked, stopping beside Lina. 'The bigger ones have more arms. But I think they're the same species. Pretty weird.'

Peering closer, she saw that he was right. The smaller stinker, the one clutching the dirty boot, had four legs and a stubby tail, with pale, leathery skin. The larger one had two more limbs, ending in snapping pincers. Its skin was darker, hard and segmented.

The big stinker lashed out and the other scrambled back, hugging the shoe to its scrawny chest. As Lina watched, the large one reared up, its mouth yawning open to reveal rows of pointed teeth.

Then, without warning, something

came shooting out. The creature's tongue was long and pink, moving like lightning as it wrapped around the boot and yanked it free.

The little stinker jumped up and down, squawking furiously, but the big stinker had the shoe now and wasn't about to let go.

'Hey, I recognise that.'

Gozetta reached down, grabbing the shoe and shaking the stinker loose. It looked up at her, screeching and puffing itself up. Gozetta aimed a kick and the stinker flew into the undergrowth with a surprised squeal. The little one smirked and scampered away.

Gozetta frowned. 'Meggin's other boot,' she said, turning it over in her hands. 'I guess that solves that mystery.' The shoe was torn from top to sole, spattered with stinker goo and a darker liquid.

'You think the . . . thing took him?' Bort asked, unable to hide the tremor in his voice.

'I certainly hope so,' Gozetta spat. 'And the same goes for the others at the lodge.'

'You . . . you hope so?' Lina asked in astonishment. 'Why?'

Gozetta smiled coldly. 'Because the other possibility is that they deserted their post and ran off into the jungle. And I can't abide cowardice.' She shot Bort a pointed stare.

Lina looked away, back down the trail towards the lodge. She'd met self-centred people before, but Gozetta took it to a whole new level.

'Up here,' a voice called. Corin was beckoning to them, further up the trail.

Above him the steep mesa loomed, rising from the greenery.

As they drew closer, Lina saw what he was pointing at. The cave was high and narrow, set deep into the side of the cliff. The entrance was wreathed in vines, clinging to the black rock overhead.

'Well that sure looks like a lair to me,' Gozetta said in a low voice, drawing her rifle.

'And it would explain why nothing showed up on your scans,' Milo agreed.

The clearing outside the cave mouth was littered with refuse left by the stinkers. Lina could see more of them in the entranceway, struggling to haul a huge cooking pot over the rocky terrain, screeching and gesturing to one another.

'What's this?' Corin asked, approaching the cliff and brushing back the vines with one bony hand. 'Look. We are not the first to find this place.'

Something had been carved into the side of the cliff, a pattern emerging as Corin swept the creepers aside. It depicted a large, crude figure with four arms and two legs, and a dagger-shaped head filled with rows of pointed teeth. Humanoid shapes cowered before it, their heads bowed.

A gust of wind whistled through the mouth of the cave, prickling the hairs on Lina's neck. 'This cave must be very old,' she whispered.

'Yes, child.' The Pau'an's blood-red lips drew back, showing sharp teeth. 'It is ancient and sacred. A place of worship.'

Lina touched the wall with the flat of her palm. Despite the heat of the day, the smooth stone felt cold.

Her parents would have loved this place, Lina thought. Sites like this were the reason the Grafs had come to Wild Space, the scratchings on a wall that might be all that remained of a once proud civilisation.

Frustration welled up inside her. Her parents were out there somewhere, in the clutches of the Empire. And here she and Milo were, wasting their time with this ridiculous hunt. But what choice did they have? They had to see it through, then maybe they could figure out who sent that transmission.

'Well I didn't come here to pray,' Gozetta snapped. 'I came here to kill.'

'So what's your big plan?' Lina asked, suddenly sick of Gozetta's selfishness and cruelty. 'Wait until it comes out, then shoot it and stick it on your wall?'

The huntress regarded the cave thoughtfully, then she shook her head. 'I don't intend to wait,' she said. 'If this thing's fed, it could be down there for days, even months.'

'Going in after it could be

dangerous,' Milo said. 'It'll be dark. You'd be on its turf, fighting blind.'

'My thoughts exactly,' Gozetta agreed. 'We need to draw it back out into the open.'

'How are you going to do that?' Milo asked.

Gozetta looked at him. 'I'll need some kind of bait,' she said. 'Small, but fast, to walk into that cave and lure the beast out. Bait that will do exactly as I say if they ever want to get off this planet alive.' She leaned in close to Milo and Lina and grinned. 'Now where would I find bait like that?'

# CHAPTER 6

## LAIR OF THE BEAST

The cavern was steep and black, damp walls shimmering in the fading light. Milo and Lina locked arms, picking their way over the rocky ground. She told him what CR-8R had said about the hyperdrive and he smiled hopefully. 'I can't wait to get off this planet.'

Lina nodded. 'You and me both,' she said. 'This cave would give me the shivers even if it wasn't for the . . . whatever it is lurking in it. And those horrible little stinkers only make it worse.'

The smell was even thicker down here, and all around they could hear the chatter and scrabble of the creatures as they divided up the spoils.

'Don't you think it's odd, though?' Milo asked. 'Why would they make their home in the lair of the planet's biggest predator?'

'Maybe they taste worse than they smell,' Lina offered.

'That would make sense,' Milo agreed, pushing through a curtain of hanging creepers. 'But I'm starting to think maybe . . . hey!'

He staggered back as something sprang at him, landing on his shoulder. Lina reached out instinctively, snatching a fallen branch and brandishing it in both hands.

But the thing didn't move, lying draped on Milo's arm. He picked at it, holding it up in the dim light. It was a flat strip of what looked like animal skin, roughly textured with four appendages.

'Amazing,' Milo said. 'This must be from the little ones. I guess they shed it when they grow those extra limbs. Fascinating.'

'Look, I know what you're going to ask, and the answer's no,' Lina said firmly. 'There's no way you're keeping the galaxy's stinkiest species for a pet. Not on my ship.'

Milo frowned. The idea had crossed his mind. The creatures seemed smart for their size, and he was beginning to hatch a theory about their bizarre life cycle.

'I'm just going to scoop up some of this,' he told Lina. 'I've got an idea.' He crouched and took off his pack, stuffing

the skin inside and pulling out a sample
jar. Lina watched in disgust as he
scooped a handful of the slimy stinker
goo into it.

'Milo, seriously,' she said. 'That's
foul. We're not down here for a
biology lesson, remember? We've got a
job to do.'

Milo got to his feet. 'I just– What have you got there?'

He gestured to the branch in Lina's hand. She looked, and in the dim light she saw that it wasn't a branch at all. It gleamed white, the curved shaft tipped by circular bumps on either end.

Looking around they could make out hundreds of similar shapes, a snaking ribcage topped by a huge, snarling skull. But the gundark was dead, left for the stinkers to pick clean. Milo could only wonder what kind of monster could have brought down one of the most vicious killers in the galaxy.

They moved on, the walls of the cave closing around them. Light filtered down through fine cracks in the roof, but Milo still wished they'd thought to bring their own light-sticks, particularly when he stubbed his toe on a rock. He let out a cry, unable to stop himself. Lina glared at him.

'Sorry,' he hissed. 'Ouch, that . . . wait, what was that?'

The sound had been distant and barely audible, even now he wasn't sure he'd heard it. Maybe it was just another of those stinkers, chattering away in the darkness.

Lina opened her mouth to speak, but shut it as the noise came again. It was a voice, somewhere deep inside the cave. Not an animal, not a monster but a human voice, calling out desperately.

'Help!' it cried, and Lina's eyes lit up. 'Help me!'

She grabbed him and they ran, scrambling over fallen rocks and scattered bones, deeper into the darkness.

They found them on the floor of a

deep, stony pit sunk several metres down into the base of the cave. Peering over the lip of the pit Milo could make out two humanoid figures, one standing and one lying, seemingly asleep.

'Help us,' the standing figure called out, reaching for them. It was a young woman with skin as pale as bone, her eyes ringed with blue. 'I can't climb up, it's too slippery.'

'We'll get you out,' Lina assured her. She turned to Milo. 'Did you bring any rope?'

He shook his head. Then he remembered. 'My net!' he said, pulling the black, pistol-shaped device from his pack. 'I think there's a way to disable the detach mechanism.'

Down in the pit the young woman crouched, shaking the second figure firmly. He groaned, rolling onto his back. It was a large man with no boots. His small, sunken eyes fluttered open.

Then he sat up suddenly, remembering. 'Sata,' he said. 'Where are we? Are we dead?'

'Don't you remember?' she asked. 'That monster stunned us with something, then the little ones dragged us in here. But look, Meggin. These children have come to help.'

The man peered up. 'Children? What children?'

Lina gave a little wave. 'Hi,' she said. 'I'm Lina and this is Milo. And you should keep your voice down if you don't want that thing to come and eat you.'

The man scowled. 'Where's Gozetta?' he demanded. 'I thought she'd come for us.'

'She's just outside,' Lina explained. 'Waiting for the thing to come out so she can kill it. We're the bait.'

'That's Gozetta all right,' the young woman frowned.

'I knew she wouldn't leave me,' Meggin said with relief. 'She'll blast this beast to smithereens then we can all go home.' Then he looked around, confused. 'Hang on, where's Delih? Where's that cursed Cerean?'

Sata bit her lip. 'It took him,' she said. 'While you were unconscious. It took him and there was nothing I could do.'

Meggin's face fell. 'I'm . . . I'm sorry,' he said. 'I didn't–'

'Okay, everyone stand back,' Milo called out, aiming with his net launcher. He squeezed the trigger and the web spiralled outward, down

into the pit. But the central thread stayed attached to the launcher in his hand, fastened tight to the locking mechanism inside the barrel.

'Now I just need to anchor this on something,' he said, heading for a tall stalagmite on the edge of the pit. He began to wind the thread around the base of the rocky pillar, but before he could make it secure he felt the rope twitching in his hands.

'Wait!' he cried out. 'I'm not ready!'

But the net launcher was jerked from his grip, skittering towards the rim of the pit. Lina lunged for it, throwing herself down just as it was about to go over the edge.

From the pit they heard a cry of pain and anger, as Meggin fell flat on his back, tangled in the net. 'Curse it, that hurt!'

And from deep below came an answering roar. It rumbled through the warm air, rising in pitch and intensity, a growl becoming a howl. Milo pressed his hands over his ears as the walls shook, pebbles rattling loose and raining down into the cavern.

'So much for staying quiet,' Lina

whispered in the silence that followed.

'It's coming,' Meggin said, jumping to his feet. 'Boy, help me out! Hurry!'

Lina handed the net launcher back to Milo and he wound it as tightly as he could around the stalagmite's sturdy base. 'Okay, climb up,' he called out.

Meggin came first, scrambling up the net. Lina took hold of his arm, helping him to climb the last few metres. He dragged himself over the lip of the pit, breathing hard. Then he sprang to his feet and began to sprint towards the cave mouth.

'I must apologise for Megs,' Sata said as she hauled herself up. 'He's had a tough day. But it would've been a lot worse if you hadn't found us.'

The roar came again, louder now and a lot closer. They could hear the scraping of claws on stone, the sound of something dragging towards them through the depths of the cave.

'We're not safe yet,' Lina said, pulling the young woman over the edge.

Milo unwound the thread, trying not to let it get tangled up.

'Milo,' Lina whispered insistently. 'We really, really need to go.'

He pulled the net launcher free, hitting the retractor button. The net began to rewind itself, spooling back into the barrel.

'Come on,' Milo whispered anxiously. Then a sound made him look up.

Something was approaching from the back of the cave, something that made the walls shake with every step. At first all Milo could see was a three-clawed hand grasping for purchase on the rock, but even in the half-light he could see that each finger of that hand was roughly as long as he was, with five knuckle joints beneath black, reflective skin.

He backed away, stumbling over stones and bones, his heart hammering. The creature's pointed head swung into view, snout first. Milo stood transfixed. He could hear the others running for the cave mouth, but he felt pinned to the spot. The creature loomed over him, lowering its vast, armoured skull.

His suspicions had been right, this was recognisably the same species as those stinkers they'd tracked up here. Their life cycle must be long and complex, and only the very toughest would make it to this terrifying final stage. But that knowledge brought him no comfort now, as he stared up in horror and amazement.

There was something insect-like

about its black exoskeleton, but it was like no bug Milo had ever seen. Its teeth were ragged, like those of a sea beast, but its tail was reptilian, writhing like a snake. Somehow the eyes were the worst of all, filled with a kind of hateful intelligence.

Then the beast's foot came down, shaking Milo from his stupor. He turned, seeing Lina up ahead, the young woman taking her hand. Milo balled his fists and bit his lip, and ran for his life.

# CHAPTER 7

## THE BEAST

Gozetta stood facing the mouth of the cave, tapping her foot impatiently. Bort and Corin had taken cover behind a pair of boulders on either side of the clearing, but Gozetta was no coward. Whatever may come, let it come.

She was starting to think this plan had been a mistake. Those children were not to be trusted. There could be another entrance to the cave for all she knew; they might already be on their way back to the landing site. Or maybe they'd blundered in there and got themselves eaten, that would be typical.

Ah well, if they had been devoured it was no great loss.

She felt a thrill of excitement. This creature was proving a challenge, she liked that. It was big and it was strong, the mess at the lodge proved that. At the time she'd been furious, but now she saw that the beast had been provoking her, laying down a challenge.

She was keeping her shuttle on standby, just in case. There was no sense taking unnecessary risks. She had a tracker locked to her belt, and at the push of a single button the ship would launch from the landing strip and make straight for her. Perhaps it was cheating, having that kind of advantage over her opponent. She preferred to think of it as insurance.

'How long are we supposed to hang around here, boss?' Bort asked, holstering his blaster. He'd tied a scarf around his face to stifle the foul smell emanating from the cave, making him look like a space-pirate in one of the old holos.

'As long as it takes,' she replied.

An unearthly sound cut the silence. It began as a rumbling deep within the cave, rising to a bellowing roar.

Good, she thought, clipping the mask over her face and feeling her senses sharpen. She rested her finger lightly on the rifle's trigger, sighting along the barrel. Game on.

Meggin burst from the cave, his face red, his bald head gleaming with sweat.

'Boss!' he cried, throwing his arms wide and stumbling towards her. 'You came for me!'

Gozetta shoved him aside. 'I'm not here for you,' she snarled, her voice muffled by the mask. 'I'm here for that.'

And she pointed into the cave where a much larger form could be glimpsed in the deep shadows, pulling itself towards them with clawed hands, teeth glinting in the half-light.

The children were barely a few paces ahead of it, their eyes wide, their legs pumping furiously as they sprinted from the opening. Sata was hurrying them along, casting a fearful glance over her shoulder as they fled into the daylight. There was no sign of the Cerean.

'Get out of here,' Lina cried, running up to Gozetta. 'It's coming!' She had no love for the huntress, but that didn't mean she wanted her to be eaten.

'I know it's coming,' Gozetta snarled. 'That was the whole point, remember?'

'But you don't understand,' Milo

told her between breaths. 'It's big. Like, really big.'

Gozetta snorted. 'I told you before,' she said. 'This is what I do. Now get out of my way.'

'You should listen to them, Gozetta,' Sata insisted. 'For once in your life, don't be a fool.'

'How dare you?' Gozetta shot back. 'Consider yourself fired.'

Sata shook her head. 'It's your life,' she said. 'Come on, you two. With any luck she'll slow it down long enough for us to get away.'

Lina and Milo followed Sata to the edge of the clearing, where the trail of destruction ran back down to the lodge far below. But Milo couldn't help looking back, ignoring Lina's firm tug on his arm.

Gozetta was gesturing to her men.

'Bort, go for the leg,' she ordered.
'Corin, for the eyes. Aim for the weak
spots.'

'What if it doesn't have any weak
spots?' Bort called back.

'Everything has weak spots,' Gozetta
told him. 'Well, except me.'

Milo felt the ground shuddering as the creature emerged from the shadows of the cave and drew itself up to full height. Gozetta planted her feet in the earth, taking careful aim at where the monster's head should be. She cursed, tilting the rifle upward, squinting in the sunlight. But her aim was still low. She peered up, and Milo saw her jaw drop open.

The monster stood over her, blocking the sun. Its head alone was the size of a shuttle. It had four reddish arms, two ending in gleaming pincers, the others in ragged claws. Its legs were taller than the trees, its feet the size of meteor craters. Its tail lashed like loose rope, slicing through the creepers covering the cave mouth.

Gozetta backed away, glancing left and right. But there was nowhere to

hide from this monster. Milo could see
the mercenaries looking at her with
terror on their faces. Would they stand
and fight, he wondered? But he knew
the answer already.

To his surprise, it was Corin who
broke first. One moment he was

staring up at the beast, his mouth and eyes wide. The next he was bolting towards Milo and Lina, his blaster forgotten, his cloak flapping out behind him.

'Where are you going?' Gozetta called out. 'You can't outrun it.'

'I don't need to outrun it,' Corin called back. 'I only need to outrun you.'

But the creature was already moving. One of the pincers swung in, latching around Corin's waist and lifting him off the ground, bellowing and kicking.

But to Milo's surprise, the creature didn't swallow Corin. It held him firm, the pincer locked around his waist. Its reptilian tail swung around, weaving and bobbing as though it had a mind of its own. Corin was transfixed, staring at the writhing serpent with wide eyes.

Then the pointed tip swept in, striking him once in the arm. Corin's eyes drooped and his head lolled backward, his whole body slackening. Milo saw a droplet of liquid gleaming on the tip of the creature's tail. Some kind of paralysing agent, he realised, and was amazed once more at the creature's resourcefulness.

The pincers snapped open and Corin dropped to the ground, unconscious. As Milo watched, the stinkers swarmed in, taking hold of the body and dragging it towards the cave. Then Lina tugged on his sleeve, and he allowed himself to be drawn away.

Gozetta looked up at the beast. Realisation hit her like a dead weight. She could not defeat this thing. In its shadow she felt smaller than an insect, and just as vulnerable. She didn't stand a chance.

The creature took a last look at Corin as he vanished into the cave mouth, then it swung back around, lowering that pointed head, its teeth gleaming in the hazy light.

The huntress shouldered her rifle, peering through the scope.
She narrowed her eyes, gritted her teeth and prepared to fire.
The creature raised one arm like a challenge, and roared.

Gozetta turned on her heel and ran.

# CHAPTER 8

## THE FIGHT

Milo and Lina were halfway down the hill when Gozetta sprinted past them, her rifle slung over her shoulder, her red hair streaming out behind. She was hammering urgently on a button fixed to her waist, and seemed to be muttering 'Come on, come on, come on,' under her breath as she ran.

'Boss!' Meggin shouted as she flew by. 'Wait for me!'

But Gozetta's pace did not flag as she shouldered past him and vanished into the trees. Lina watched her go, grasping Milo's hand and trying to keep up.

'She's changed . . . her tune,' she

managed between breaths.

'Maybe ... she's not so dumb ... after all,' Milo panted, and grinned.

Sata frowned at them. 'Less talk,' she said. 'More running.'

They could hear trees splintering as the beast tracked them through the jungle. Lina wondered what could have happened to Bort. Had he managed to flee, like Gozetta? Then for a moment the footsteps paused, and in the silence that followed she heard a distant cry, abruptly cut off.

They broke out onto open ground and now they could see the hunting lodge below them, shimmering in the sunlight. Something hung in the sky above it. Lina recognised Gozetta's golden shuttle, hovering on its thrusters. She could see the huntress up ahead, dashing towards the sleek little craft.

Meggin picked up the pace, his red face beaming. 'We're saved!' he cried out. 'We're right behind you, boss!' He turned back to Milo and Lina. 'Look, children, we're saved!'

'Don't bet on it,' Sata growled, but she put on a burst of speed nonetheless. Lina struggled after her, wondering how long they could keep up this punishing pace.

The ship descended, rocking on a current of air. The hatch began to lower as Gozetta drew closer. She leaped, grabbing on and hauling herself over the lip. Then she vanished inside and the hatch began to close.

'She'll pick us up, just you watch.' Meggin said.

The ship righted itself. Lina could see Gozetta in the cockpit, strapping herself in and taking the helm. She glanced back at them, then looked away.

In that moment Lina knew that Meggin's hopes were false. Gozetta would not risk her life for them. She gave them a single, apologetic wave, and hit the thrusters.

'No!' Meggin cried out. 'No, wait!'

But his words were drowned out by a deafening scream as the ship began to rise. Dust clouds erupted and Lina had to cover her eyes as they were blasted with heat. The engines roared.

And the jungle roared back.

The creature rose from the forest, perched atop one of the tallest trees. It clung on with its lower limbs and raised its pincered arms to the sky. Lina saw it silhouetted against the sun, cut out in black like something from the darkest nightmare.

Despite herself, she almost laughed. They'd come here looking for safe haven, but found themselves in deeper trouble than before. Evading stormtroopers was fun compared to this. She almost wished Captain Korda had tracked them here, so she could see the look in his eyes when he came face to face with this monster.

The creature sprang for the shuttle, lashing out with one vast claw and knocking the ship aside. The noise of the engines changed from a low rumble to a high, protesting whine as Gozetta fought for control, her face whitening as she saw the creature rearing up on its haunches and grabbing again.

Pincers locked around the rear engine port, pulling the ship backward. The thrusters fired, blasting hot gas into the beast's face. It let out a howl of pain, its snout blackened and blistered. But it did not let go, tearing at the shuttle with its great claws. Clouds of steam billowed as pipes were severed and systems began to fail.

'We should go,' Milo said. 'Now, while it's distracted.'

Lina nodded, dashing after him down the slope, unable to tear her eyes from the spectacle up ahead. Gozetta had managed to train one of her aft cannons on the creature, hitting it with a spray of laser fire. One of its claw arms hung, useless, but the other three reached in, tearing and clawing with furious energy.

They reached the track that led down to the *Whisper Bird* and there they paused, breathing hard. Lina pulled the transmitter from her pocket, flicking it on.

'Crater,' she cried out. 'Crater, can you hear me?'

'Oh, Mistress Lina!' CR-8R's overjoyed voice came back. 'Myself and Morq were so concerned for your–'

'Not now,' Lina shouted, glancing back up the hill to see the creature's tail wrapping around the shuttle and squeezing tight. Struts snapped and smoke hissed as the engines continued to roar and whine. 'We're on our way. Get the *Whisper Bird* prepped and ready to fly!'

'The couplings are on board but the hyperdrive isn't entirely . . .'

'Forget that,' Lina told him. 'We need to get off-world, fast. We can finish fixing it in orbit.'

'Very well,' CR-8R said. 'Would you like me to come and pick you up?'

Lina looked back towards the lodge. 'I really don't think that's wise,' she said. 'There's . . . something after us. But don't worry, we'll find a way to shake it off.'

'Mistress Lina, are you in danger?' CR-8R asked. 'If you are, it's in my programming to assist you in whatever way I can.'

'We'll be okay, Crater,' Lina insisted. 'Stay where you are and keep the engines warm. We'll be right there.' She flicked off the transmitter.

Milo pointed excitedly. 'Look,' he said. 'I think Gozetta's going to make it.'

He was right. Somehow, the shuttle had broken free of the creature's grasp and was rising, rocking unsteadily as it ascended, firing on only two thrusters but it seemed to be enough. Through the cockpit glass Lina could see a pale, determined figure fighting with the controls as the ship cleared the trees.

Then the creature made a last, wild leap. Its mouth yawned open in mid-air and from within came a huge, wet shape, moving faster than a bowcaster bolt. The tongue shot out, wrapping around the ship and dragging it back. The ship span, engines firing madly in all directions.

The creature's jaws closed around the shuttle. Then it tumbled free, crashing into the trees and bursting into flames. The monster screeched with pain, swatting at its wounded mouth. The ship rolled, branches shattering as it came to a smoking halt.

Lina felt suddenly exposed, out here on the track leading down to the landing field.

'We can't stop here,' Sata urged. 'We have to find somewhere to hide.'

'We have a ship,' Lina told her. 'Down

on the landing field.'

Meggin's eyes lit up. 'A ship?' he asked. 'Why didn't you say?'

'Wait,' Milo said, wriggling out of his backpack. 'I've got an idea, but we have to stay still for it to work.'

The creature's great head swung towards them. For a moment it watched, motionless, its black eyes gleaming. Then it took a step towards them.

'Forget that,' Meggin said. 'You stay if you like. If there's a way off this planet, I'm taking it.'

He hurtled off down the track.

Lina looked at Milo apologetically. 'I'm sure it's a great plan,' she said. 'But we don't have a choice. Run!'

They plunged down the muddy trail towards the landing strip. The air grew thick with mist, hot and humid. Lina was almost too tired to be frightened any more, but the sounds of the creature behind them gave her speed. It came blundering along the track, its strides shaking the ground.

'Move, both of you!' Sata yelled, shoving them forward as a massive foot fell behind her and a clawed hand swept the air overhead. Lina could hear the beast breathing, could see its red eyes smoking like beacons in the fog. They were in its shadow now, and it was only a matter of time before it–

'You there!' a voice echoed up ahead, piercingly loud. 'Yes, you. Stop right there!'

A bright light sliced through the mist and the creature skidded to an abrupt halt.

# CHAPTER 9

## MILO'S PLAN

M ilo threw himself forward, joining Meggin on the edge of the landing field. The creature had stopped, sniffing the air. He could hear it growling, sweeping with its mighty pincered arms.

Twin beams illuminated the gloom and the voice boomed out again. 'By the authority vested in me, I demand that you cease and desist all illegal pursuit, and return at once to the hole from whence you came!'

Milo could hear the creature whining uncertainly, unable to discern this new threat either by scent or sight. It took a step back, snapping its jaws defensively.

Then a thin wind blew and the mist broke up, and they saw the owner of the voice. CR-8R floated a few metres above the landing field, his arms outstretched, his glowlamps on high beam. He would have looked almost impressive if it hadn't been for the sheer size of the monster looming over him. In its mighty

shadow he was little more than a toy.

'Listen to me,' the droid called out, his vocabulator turned to full strength. 'I command you to halt!'

Milo could just make out the shape of the *Whisper Bird* up ahead – if they ran, they might make it. But what about CR-8R? They couldn't leave him.

There was only one thing for it. He'd have to put his plan into action.

'Quickly, all of you,' he said, rooting around in his pack and pulling out the sticky sample jar. 'We have to put this stuff on.'

He unscrewed the lid, handing the jar to Lina. She scooped out a handful of slime, grimacing. 'Are you sure?' she asked.

'No,' Milo admitted. 'But it's the only plan we've got. The six arms, the tongue, it all makes sense. That thing up there is just one massive stinker. They go through all these different phases, and that is the end result.'

'That's ridiculous,' Meggin said. 'If that were true, why aren't there more of these ... beasts?'

'Because it doesn't want any rivals,' Milo argued. 'It's fine with them when they're little, they help it catch food and in return they get to pick the bones. But I'll bet that as soon as they're big enough to be a threat, it kills them off. But the point is, it doesn't eat the little ones. And if we smell like they do ...'

Sata smeared the grey goop all over her face and arms before passing the jar to Meggin. He frowned at Milo, then heard a bellow from behind them and did as he was told.

The creature had circled towards CR-8R, fascinated by him but still

unwilling to attack. The droid was
waving his arms and flashing his beams,
spinning on his repulsors and trying
everything he could to appear bigger,
weirder and more dangerous than he
really was.

'Go home!' he was shouting. 'Back to
your cave! You're getting very tired! Very
sleepy!'

The droid dodged aside as one of
the monster's feet thudded down just
centimetres from him.

'Hey, there's no need for that!' CR-8R
called out. 'I demand that you–'

The other foot slammed down and
CR-8R swerved just in time, taking a
glancing blow on the arm.

'You're being most unreasonable!'
he managed, then one of the pincers
struck him in the side and he rolled,
splashing into the muck. The creature

lunged after him.

'Enough!' CR-8R cried, but the monster's foot came down and he was crushed into the mud, one loose limb spiralling free. Milo heard Lina gasp, felt her clutch his arm.

Then the creature turned on them and all other concerns dropped away. Its eyes glowed like twin flames as it approached, stalking step by step.

They froze.

Boom, doom. The monster lumbered closer, lowering its vast snout. Milo clutched Lina's hand. He wanted badly to close his eyes but he knew he couldn't. He tried to keep his breathing shallow as the shadow fell over them and the footsteps ceased their thunder. The creature's tail slapped in the mud. He could feel its hot, damp breath on his face.

Something touched Milo on the top of his head and he flinched. It trickled down into his face, stinking of rotting meat, and he realised the monster had drooled on him. He fought the urge to wipe it away, holding perfectly still as the great snout came into view.

He could feel Lina's hand trembling, was dimly aware of Sata at his side. Meggin had begun to whimper. 'Go away,' he squeaked, sounding more like a

scared child than a grown man. 'Please, go away.'

'Hush,' Lina hissed, as loudly as she dared. 'You'll get us all killed.'

Then she shut her mouth quickly as the creature lowered its head, crouching until its wet, bulging eye was level with her face. The eye moved on to Milo and he felt the monster staring into him, scanning every centimetre. His only hope was that, like other predatory creatures, it would trust scent over sight.

The creature sniffed again, giving a little grunt of disappointment. Then the head was gone, raising on its long neck. Milo took a breath, trying to stay calm, to stay still. The monster opened its mouth, its tongue unrolling. The tip twitched, lowering until it was barely centimetres above Milo's head.

Then there was a boom, and a roar. Something struck the creature, rippling with fire. It let out a howl, turning and snapping. The hard shell on its back cracked.

The creature lumbered in a circle, scanning the trees for the source of its pain. Milo's breath caught in his throat as he saw a bedraggled figure in the distance, a rocket launcher balanced on her shoulder. Gozetta's face was black with soot and streaked with blood, but she stood upright, facing down her enemy.

'Come on!' she shouted, her voice amplified by the mask over her mouth. 'You and me, right now!'

The creature lowered its snout and let out a bellow of rage. Then it pounded towards Gozetta, every footstep an earthquake. She fired off another

projectile, but the monster dodged. The
rocket hit the ground, sending up a spray
of mud and steam and fire.

Gozetta backed into the trees and the
creature followed, smashing through the
foliage with a crash and a roar.

Then there was silence.

# CHAPTER 10

## A NEW DESTINATION

They found CR-8R face up in the mud, gazing into the sky and buzzing quietly. Lina helped him up and he swayed unsteadily on his repulsors, his body weighed down with a thick coating of grime.

'Thank you, Mistress Lilo,' he said. 'I'm door I'll be all bite in a short crime.'

'You'll be fine, Crate,' Lina assured him, scraping the worst of the gunk from his metallic face. 'You've just had a bit of a knock.'

'You saved our lives, you know,' Milo told the droid, picking up the loose limb and handing it to CR-8R. 'That thing would've had us if you hadn't distracted it.'

CR-8R let out a satisfied hum, and Lina could have sworn he was smiling. 'That's kind of you to say, Master Lina,' he said. 'But it's in my programming to protect you, whatever the risk to my own wife.'

Morq came scurrying from the *Whisper Bird* to greet them, splashing joyfully past Sata and Meggin, making straight for Milo. The boy grinned, holding out his hands.

A roar echoed from the jungle behind them. Morq turned tail and fled back to the *Bird*, screeching and chattering.

'We need to get out of here,' Lina said, picking up the pace.

'Do you think she's got a chance?' Milo asked, gesturing out into the dense forest.

Lina shrugged. 'Her and that thing, they're both as mad as each other,' she said. 'So maybe.'

The access ramp lowered and she strode into the cargo bay, folding out the passenger seats as CR-8R and Milo hurried up into the cockpit. Meggin clipped on his belt, casting an uncertain glance through the open hatchway door.

'I ought to say thank you,' he said awkwardly. 'I mean, I want to. You and Milo, you saved my life. I won't forget it. If there's ever anything I can do . . . '

Lina nodded shyly. 'It was nothing,' she said. 'You would've done the same for us. Right?'

Meggin looked unsure, then he nodded. 'Right,' he said.

Lina climbed the ladder into the

cockpit. CR-8R floated in his usual spot, his arms whipping and whirring as he connected cables, disconnected others and tapped the navicom controls.

'Where are we going?' Milo asked. 'We never did find the source of the transmission.'

Lina frowned. 'Not so loud,' she whispered, nodding towards the rear hangar.

'But maybe she sent it,' Milo quietly pointed out. 'Maybe she could help us.'

'It's too risky,' Lina told him. 'For now, let's just get into orbit. Crater, you said the hyperdrive still needs work.'

'An hour, no more,' CR-8R reassured her as the thrusters roared and the *Whisper Bird* began to rise. 'We'll be out of this system before you know it.'

* * *

'An hour,' Lina found herself muttering bitterly as they circled the planet some time later. 'More like five.'

She crouched in the cargo bay, up to her neck in wires. CR-8R drifted back and forth overhead, letting out a stream of complaints and computer code. The *Venture*'s hyperdrive couplings were stubbornly refusing to polarise, or to interlink with the *Whisper Bird*'s outdated systems.

One by one Milo, Lina, Sata and Meggin had taken the time to use the cramped little washroom, scrubbing themselves clean of that foul, reeking slime. But the smell was still thick in the cabin, clinging to their clothes, the seats, everything. That was the problem with recycled air, Lina thought. If only they could open a window – but in high orbit, that wasn't really a good idea.

'Mistress Lina, see if you can run the sector 7 out-lead into the naviscope array,' CR-8R suggested, peering down. 'That might give the polarisers a boost.'

Lina did as she was told, jerking back as sparks exploded from the wall. 'I don't think they're compatible, Crater,' she said.

CR-8R let out an electronic sigh. 'Very well,' he said. 'Back to square one. Curse this hyperdrive and all its rusty little circuits.'

Milo passed Lina a hot cup of caf, serving the others before settling into an empty seat and letting out a long, loud yawn.

'How long is it since you've slept?' Sata asked, looking at him with concern.

'I don't remember,' Milo admitted, rubbing his eyes.

'I have to ask,' the Umbaran began cautiously. 'What are you kids doing all the way out here on your own?'

Milo shot Lina a quick glance, but she shook her head.

'We got lost,' she told Sata. 'We were in convoy with our parents on the way to Thune when we had a hyperdrive malfunction. But we know the way now. They'll be waiting for us.'

Sata gave her a long, thoughtful look. 'I'm sorry,' she said. 'But I can spot a liar, Lina. You might have convinced me if I hadn't heard you before, in the cockpit. Milo asked where you were going, and he said something about a transmission.'

Lina glared at Milo. 'Sorry, sis,' he said sheepishly.

'The thing is, I think I know the transmission you mean,' Sata went on. 'I wasn't the one who set up the relay. I mean, I did, but it was Delih's idea. And now he's ... he didn't ... '

'I'm sorry,' Lina said. 'He was your friend?'

'For many years,' Sata said, hanging her head. 'It was his suggestion we take this job. I was the tech expert, he designed and built the lodge. I knew he was involved in something he didn't want the authorities to know about, though he never spoke of it. I suppose he was afraid of getting me involved. Or of someone else finding out.'

Lina glanced over at Meggin, who was listening, his eyes half-closed.

'Don't worry about Megs,' Sata said, smiling at the big man. 'The three of us worked together for years, I know he's got a good heart, deep down.'

Meggin grunted. 'Thanks, pal,'
he said.

'And besides, we owe you our lives,'
Sata said. 'Where I come from, that's
a sacred trust. So tell me, what's really
going on here?'

Milo started the story and Lina
finished it, telling Sata why they were
out in Wild Space, what the Empire
had done to their parents and how
their efforts to find safe harbour had
been betrayed back on Thune. They
told her how they'd stumbled over the
transmissions, heard their call to resist
the Empire and come in search of the
source.

'So that's what Delih was doing,'
Sata said when they had finished.
'I'm glad you told me. Maybe it's for
the best the transmissions stopped,

though. I can just imagine Gozetta's face if the Empire had turned up on her doorstep, accusing her of being in league with insurgents.'

'But if this isn't the point of origin,' Milo asked, 'where is?'

Sata hesitated. 'This is a dangerous world you're getting into, children,' she said. 'The people who made those broadcasts, I don't think they're playing around.'

Lina fixed her with a firm stare. 'Neither are we,' she said. 'We have to find our parents, and the Empire aren't about to help us. Who else will?'

Sata nodded slowly. 'Very well,' she said. 'I don't know who sent the original transmissions, but I can hazard a guess. I know Delih had friends on a planet called Lothal, in the Outer Rim. I don't know much about it, except that the

Empire have a base there. Whenever he went, Delih would find some excuse to go alone.'

'We have to go there,' Lina said firmly.

'But what about that Imperial base?' Milo asked. 'We can't just land and start asking people where the nearest rebel broadcast station is.'

'We can disguise the *Bird* somehow,' Lina insisted. 'Crater can mask the ship's code. We have to try.'

'I thought you said we'd taken enough risks,' Milo countered.

Lina hung her head. 'I just want them back,' she said wearily. 'I just want to know where they are. And this is the best chance we've got.'

Milo was silent for a moment, then he nodded. 'Okay, Sis,' he said. 'You're right.'

'This Lothal,' Lina asked Sata. 'Will you take us there?'

For a long time the young woman did not speak. Then she slowly shook her head. 'You're not the only one I owe a debt to,' she said. 'Whether she meant to or not, Gozetta saved our lives too. And those mercenaries don't deserve to be left in that pit to die. Besides, neither of us have been paid yet.'

'Good point,' Meggin muttered.

'You want us to go back?' Lina asked.

'No,' Sata said. 'Just take Meggin and me to Gozetta's ship in orbit. We'll pick them up, and you can be on your way.'

Lina looked at her. 'Are you sure you wouldn't rather come with us?' she asked. 'You could help us find the people who sent the transmissions.'

Sata sighed. 'I just want to do my work, collect my pay and go back to my homeworld. I don't think I'll be leaving it again for a very long time.'

There was a long silence. Then CR-8R let out a whistle of triumph and span around on his repulsors. 'I have it,' he said. 'Mistress Lina, Master Milo, we are back in business. The hyperdrive is linked in and awaiting coordinates.'

Milo grinned up at him. 'Crater, you're amazing.'

CR-8R stopped spinning and looked

down at him. 'Yes, I am,' he said. 'And don't you forget it. Now, Miss Sata, did I hear you mention the name Lothal?'

TO BE CONTINUED IN

**STAR WARS**

ADVENTURES IN WILD SPACE

**Book Three: THE STEAL**